DC
SUPER
-VILLAINS

THE JOKER ™

AN
ORIGIN STORY

STONE ARCH BOOKS
a capstone imprint

DC Super-Villains Origins
are published by Stone Arch Books,
A Capstone Imprint
1710 Roe Crest Drive
North Mankato, Minnesota 56003
www.mycapstone.com

STAR41128

Cataloging-in-Publication Data is available on the Library of Congress website.
ISBN: 978-1-4965-7935-5 (library binding)
ISBN: 978-1-4965-8099-3 (paperback)
ISBN: 978-1-4965-7940-9 (eBook)

Summary: How did the Joker become Batman's archenemy? Discover the story behind the
Clown Prince of Crime's journey from small-time crook to big-time baddie.

Contributing artists: Erik Doescher, Mike DeCarlo, David Tanguay,
Mike Cavallaro, and Ethen Beavers
Designed by Hilary Wacholz

Printed in the United States of America.
102018 000048

DC SUPER-VILLAINS

AN ORIGIN STORY

WRITTEN BY
LOUISE SIMONSON

ILLUSTRATED BY
LUCIANO VECCHIO

BATMAN CREATED BY
BOB KANE WITH BILL FINGER

Minutes to midnight, a thick fog rolls into Gotham City.

A thief known as the Red Hood sneaks toward the Monarch Playing Card Company. He breaks the lock on the factory's door and steps inside.

BWEE-OO! BWEE-OO! An alarm rings out.

The Red Hood does not worry. He knows the safe is hidden in a nearby office.

He dashes toward the safe.

The thief is skilled at breaking all types of locks. He will be gone before the Gotham City police arrive.

CLICK! The safe opens easily.

Money spills out in front of the Red Hood.

Suddenly, the criminal hears footsteps. He looks around.

The police cannot be here already, he thinks. *It is too soon!*

The Red Hood see a figure swinging down from the ceiling. The man wears a dark uniform and a long cape.

"Batman!" the Red Hood growls.

The thief sprints out the back door of the office and down a hall. He enters a room filled with large tanks of bubbling chemicals.

The Red Hood hears Batman's footsteps behind him.

The Red Hood climbs a ladder onto a metal walkway. He turns to look for Batman but trips. The thief falls over the walkway's railing.

"Ah!" the Red Hood screams.

SPA-LOOSH! He lands in one of the chemical tanks.

The thief holds his breath in the bubbling liquid. *I'll stay here until Batman is gone,* he thinks.

When Batman finally leaves, the thief climbs out of the tank.

Chemicals drip from his clothing, hair, and skin.

The chemicals have changed him. They have turned his skin white and his hair green. His mouth is now an evil red grin.

The Red Hood sees his new face in the glass of a nearby window. He is both shocked and amazed.

I look like a clown, he thinks. Like the Joker in a deck of cards!

At that moment, the thief decides to become the Joker! He will strike fear into the people of Gotham City.

He will be Batman's greatest enemy.
He will make Batman pay for turning
him into a clown!

As part of his new identity, the Joker creates a special suit. He makes gadgets and weapons to fill its pockets.

The Joker invents a flower that squirts poison gas and a buzzer that shocks people.

He makes razor-sharp playing cards and exploding toys!

The thief even creates a dangerous type of laughing gas: Joker Venom.

After several crimes, the Joker quickly becomes Gotham City's most wanted super-villain.

Batman tracks his every move on his high-tech Batcomputer.

"You'll never catch me!" the Joker laughs.

24

For his biggest crime, the Joker plans to dump Joker Venom into Gotham City's drinking water.

FWOOSH! Batman swings in on his Batrope.

This time, the super hero stops the villain before he gets away!

The Gotham City police send the Joker to a prison called Arkham Asylum.

No cell can hold this villain for long. He is skilled at breaking locks, after all.

Soon the Joker escapes!

He flees the prison atop a giant, flying joker card.

The super-villain's crime spree has just begun.

Sometimes the Joker plans his crimes for money.

He robs banks and jewelry stores for cold, hard cash.

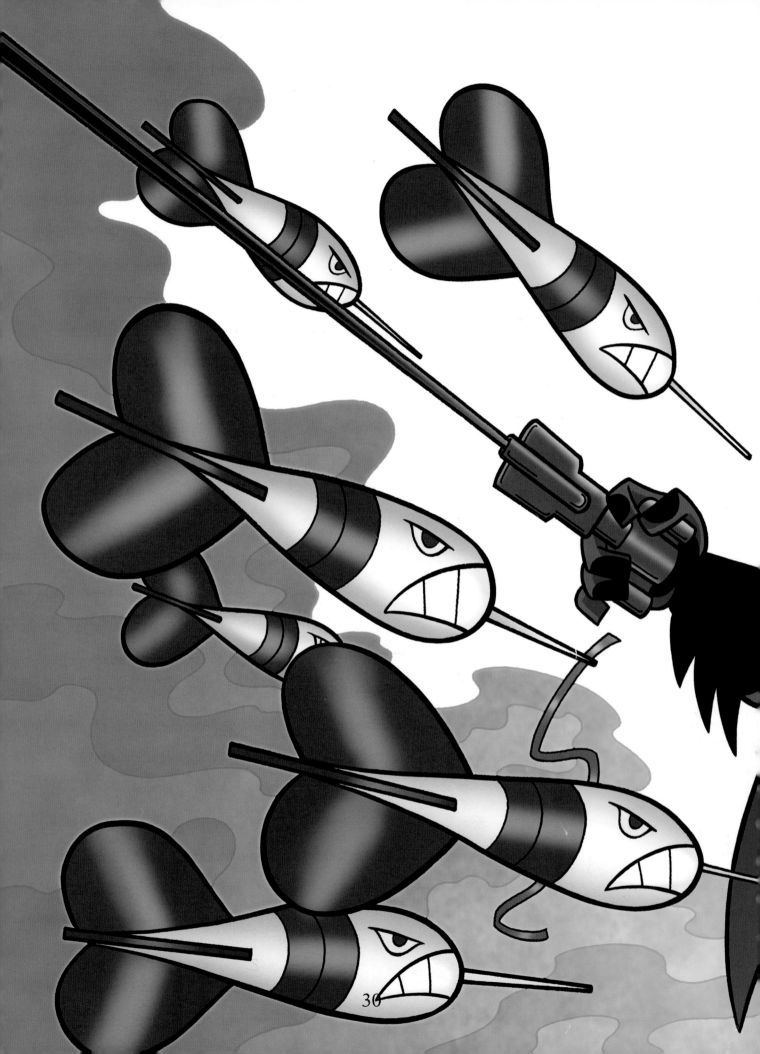

Other times the Joker creates trouble just for fun!

The villain fills colorful balloons with laughing gas. Then he uses funny-faced darts to pop them over Gotham City!

The best crimes are both fun and rewarding! the Joker thinks.

The Joker drives to the Gotham City Bank in his Jokermobile. He clicks a button on the vehicle's control panel.

A giant boxing glove appears from under the hood. *WHAM-O!* It smashes into the side of the bank. Money spills into the street.

"HAHAHA!" the Joker laughs.

After each crime, Batman sends the Joker back to Arkham Asylum.

While there, he meets the woman who will become his partner in crime, Dr. Harleen Quinzel.

She is a psychiatrist. She is supposed to help the Joker stop committing crimes.

Instead, Dr. Quinzel becomes friends with the mad criminal. She helps him escape from Arkham Asylum once again.

Dr. Quinzel decides to join the Joker in his life of crime.

She calls herself Harley Quinn. The villain creates a black and red jester costume.

Harley Quinn helps the Joker paint smiley faces on Gotham City statues. She calls the Joker her "Puddin'" and loves his crazy sense of humor!

Along with Harley, the Joker builds a secret hideout. He fills his funhouse with halls of mirrors and deadly booby traps. He has a space to park his Jokermobile!

The Joker teams up with other super-villains like the Penguin, the Riddler, Two-Face, and even Superman's enemy Lex Luthor.

Most villains don't trust the Joker. He is too dangerous, they say. They believe he will stop at nothing to get his revenge on Batman.

The Joker says, "I could never destroy Batman. That would ruin all the fun!"

But the villain promises to always get the last laugh.

EVERYTHING ABOUT . . .

THE JOKER ™

REAL NAME: UNKNOWN

CRIMINAL NAME: THE JOKER

ROLE: SUPER-VILLAIN

BASE: GOTHAM CITY

The Clown Prince of Crime. The Harlequin of Hate. The Ace of Knaves. The Joker is known by many names. But ever since a toxic bath changed this small-time crook into a big-time baddie, the Joker has only one purpose in life . . . to destroy Batman.

THE AUTHOR

LOUISE SIMONSON writes about monsters, science fiction and fantasy characters, and super heroes. She wrote the award-winning Power Pack series, several best-selling X-Men titles, Web of Spider-man for Marvel Comics, and Superman: Man of Steel and Steel for DC Comics. She has also written many books for kids. She is married to comic artist and writer Walter Simonson and lives in the suburbs of New York City.

THE ILLUSTRATOR

LUCIANO VECCHIO currently lives in Buenos Aires, Argentina. With experience in illustration, animation, and comics, his works have been published in the US, Spain, UK, France, and Argentina. His credits include Ben 10 (DC Comics), Cruel Thing (Norma), Unseen Tribe (Zuda Comics), Sentinels (Drumfish Productions), and several DC Super Heroes books for Capstone.

GLOSSARY

booby trap (BOO-bee TRAP)—hidden dangers that are set off when someone touches them

chemical (KEM-uh-kuhl)—dangerous liquids or gases often used by scientists

gadget (GAJ-it)—small tools that do a certain job

identity (eye-DEN-ti-tee)—who a person is

jester (JES-tur)—a person who often entertained kings and queens long ago

liquid (LIK-wid)—a wet substance that can be poured

psychiatrist (sye-KYE-uh-trist)—a doctor who treats emotional and mental illnesses

uniform (YOO-nuh-form)—a special set of clothes worn for a particular job

villain (VIL-uhn)—a wicked person

DISCUSSION QUESTIONS

Write down your answers. Refer back to the story for help.

QUESTION 1.

Why do you believe the Joker chose his super-villain name? Can you find any clues in the text or illustrations to support your answer?

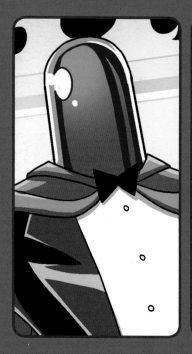 

QUESTION 2.

Which villain identity do you think is more frightening—the Red Hood or the Joker? Explain your answer.

QUESTION 3.

Several villains appear in the illustration on page 41. Who do you believe is the most powerful, and why?

QUESTION 4.

What is your favorite illustration in this book? Explain how you made your decision.

READ THEM ALL!!

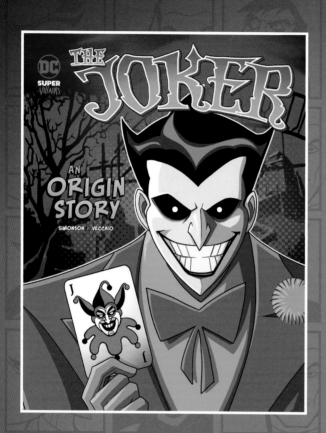

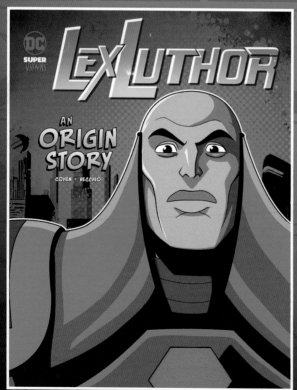

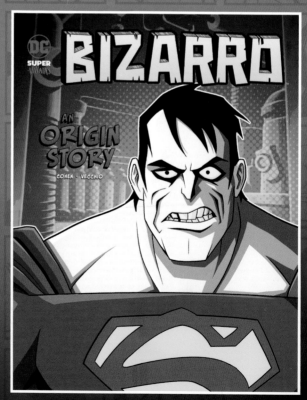